# Hero

AN
ORCA
YOUNG
READER

# Hero

## martha attema

ORCA BOOK PUBLISHERS

**National Library of Canada Cataloguing in Publication Data**
Attema, Martha, 1949-

Hero / Martha Attema.

"An Orca young reader."

ISBN 1-55143-251-X

'     I. Title.

PS8551.T74H47 2003    jC813'.54    C2003-910877-5

PZ7.A8664H47 2003

*Library of Congress Catalog Card Number:* 2003107505

Summary: In the last cold winter of WWII, Izaak is sent from hiding in Amsterdam to live on a farm in the north of Holland.

Teachers' guide available at www.orcabook.com

Orca Book Publishers gratefully acknowledges the support of its publishing programs provided by the following agencies: the Department of Canadian Heritage, the Canada Council for the Arts, and the British Columbia Arts Council.

Cover design by Christine Toller
Cover illustration by James Bentley
Interior illustrations by Stephen McCallum
Printed and bound in Canada

Orca Book Publishers is proud to demonstrate its commitment to the responsible use of our natural resources. This book is printed on Bioprint Paper supplied by Transcontinental Printing. Bioprint paper is 100% recycled, 100% post-consumer waste, processed chlorine-free, 100% Ancient-Forest free, and acid-free, using soy based inks.

*IN CANADA*
Orca Book Publishers
1030 North Park Street
Victoria, BC  Canada
V8T 1C6

*IN THE UNITED STATES*
Orca Book Publishers
PO Box 468
Custer, WA  USA
98240-0468

05 04 03 • 5  4  3  2  1

*In memory of Jan Hoogterp, my great uncle
and proud owner of Held (Hero).*

*Acknowlededgments*

Many people have encouraged me to write this story and I am grateful for their suggestions and ideas.

Thanks to Marla J. Hayes for her honesty as a friend and fellow writer; to Betty Jane Wylie for "walking" me through the difficult part; to the members of the North Bay Children's Writers' Group for their insight and suggestions; to Jan de Vries for his invaluable comments and for sharing his real-life, war-time experiences as a young boy on a farm in Friesland; to Maggie de Vries, my editor, for her patience and expert guidance during the revision process; to my father, Willie Hoogterp, for providing the detailed information about his war experience and about Held; and to Albert for always being there for me.

# The Hiding Place

*Vroom! Vroom!*

The sound of engines startled eight-year-old Izaak out of his world of make believe. He was pretending that he was the milkman, delivering milk bottles to the houses along the canal. Every chair was a house. First he loaded his metal wagon full of imaginary bottles from the dairy. Bessie, his metal horse, pulled the wagon. Izaak chatted with the people along the way. "How is the war going? Did you hear the Allied troops have liberated the southern part of the Netherlands?"

Izaak pretended to ring a bell. "Ding, ding. The milkman is here."

Outside, brakes squealed.

"Quick, Izaak, take your horse and wagon and run upstairs!" Mama stood in the doorway. The doorway of a small, gabled house. A house in Amsterdam, the Netherlands. A house that was not Izaak's.

Izaak picked up the brown, metal horse and scrambled to his feet. He thrust the little wagon in his pocket and glanced at Mama, his eyes dark with fear. Not again, he thought, and ran as quietly as he could up a second flight of stairs.

Mama was right behind him. They slipped into a room in the attic and Mama closed the door without a sound.

Izaak heard a loud knock on the front door. Footsteps sounded in the hallway. The front door creaked open.

Voices traveled up from downstairs, loud voices that made Izaak cringe.

Along the wall of their attic room

stood a large, mahogany dresser. It had been moved away from the wall. In the faint afternoon light, Izaak and Mama crept behind the dresser, through a hole cut in the wall into their secret hiding place. Together they dragged the dresser against the wall to hide the opening.

The space was just big enough for a mattress. In the corner stood a bucket that they used for a toilet. Izaak did not like the smell of that bucket.

Mama pulled him down beside her on the mattress. Her arms wound tightly around him. Izaak wriggled. He could hardly breathe.

"Shh. Not a sound," she whispered.

He felt the cold metal of the horse in his left hand. He pressed the little wagon in his pocket with his other.

Izaak and Mama sat still, as still as they could. They waited.

The sound of heavy footsteps on the stairs made Izaak shiver. Mama held him.

Her head rested on his. He smelled her warm skin. The pounding of Izaak's and Mama's heartbeats filled their small hiding place. Izaak felt the tightness of her arms.

The voices grew louder. He tried not to listen.

Now the voices had reached the room in the attic, their room. He heard the door open.

"Who are you hiding in here?" The voice of a German soldier cut through the wall.

Izaak stopped breathing. Mama stopped breathing.

"I told you, there is nobody in here," Mrs. Waterman answered.

A white line of light appeared on the floor. The beam moved from left to right and back. A flashlight, Izaak thought. Someone opened the dresser drawers, one at the time, and closed them with a bang.

The heavy footsteps trooped out the door and down the stairs.

In a long gush, Izaak and Mama blew out the air that had been stuck by fear. Izaak knew he wasn't allowed to move until Mrs. Waterman came upstairs and told them it was safe.

"Mama," he whispered, "are they gone?"

"Not yet." Mama's voice was very soft.

Izaak felt trapped, not just in his mother's arms, but in this house. In this city. In this war.

For over a year, Mama and Izaak had been in hiding at Mrs. Waterman's house.

Izaak, his twelve-year-old sister, Sarah, and their parents had lived in their own gabled house along one of Amsterdam's canals. The house had big, bright rooms. Izaak and Sarah each had their own room with sunny windows on the third floor. Izaak's room had a high ceiling and cream-painted walls. Beside his bed stood a wooden chest full of toys. Oak-stained shelves

held his favorite books and his col-
lection of metal and wooden horses.
Izaak often thought about his room and
wondered if he and his family would
ever go back there to live.

Since the war started four years ago,
things had gone from bad to worse for
Izaak's family. Not just for Izaak's family,
but for all the Jewish people in the country.

First, the German soldiers had closed
his father's jewelry store. Izaak remembered how angry Papa had been and
how Mama had cried. Then they'd moved
from their bright house to a small
apartment above a warehouse. Living
in the apartment became too dangerous when the Germans had ordered
them to live in the ghetto. The Jews
were forced to live together, so it was
easier for the Nazis to hunt them down.
From the ghetto, Jewish people were
sent to camps in Germany and Poland.
Papa said the people were herded onto
trains like cattle.

"We are disobeying this order." Papa

had ripped up the paper and thrown the pieces in the stove. "We are not going to live in the ghetto. We are not going to be sent on trains to the camps. We will go into hiding until this war is over. I have contacts."

Izaak trembled. Friends from school had left on those trains to camps in Germany. He was glad his father had suggested they go into hiding.

"Mama," Izaak whispered now, "tell me again about the yellow star."

"Oh, Izaak." Mama dropped a kiss on his head. "A man named Hitler, the leader of Germany, wants to rule the whole world."

Izaak nodded. He knew, but didn't understand how Hitler could fight all the countries in the world. He had seen the soldiers though. He'd watched them march in the streets. Every day, he saw military trucks loaded with soldiers. And here, Papa had told him, in the city of Amsterdam, were thousands and thousands of soldiers.

"Hitler doesn't like Jews. He wants to lock them up." Mama paused. "Or send them away."

"Why Jews?"

"Because Hitler blames the Jews for all the bad things that happen in Germany." Mama sighed; her eyes filled with tears.

Izaak found it hard to believe that the Jews could cause so much trouble that Hitler wanted to get rid of the Jewish population in all of Europe.

"He also wants to make sure everybody will recognize the Jews. That's why we all have to wear the Star of David on our coats."

Izaak nodded. Papa had told him he should be proud to be Jewish. But he was scared to be recognized.

"Can we leave now?" Izaak whispered.

"Not yet. We have to wait till Mrs. Waterman comes upstairs. She'll tell us when it's safe."

Izaak wriggled in his mother's arms. He closed his eyes and tried to think of Papa and Sarah. He remembered his father's strong arms. When Izaak was little, Papa had carried him up the stairs every night. At first, when he closed his eyes tight, he could see his father's face: those dark eyes that sparkled when he laughed, the bushy eyebrows that frowned and made a straight line when he was cross. Lately, Izaak found it harder to remember what Papa looked like. He hadn't seen his father for over a year. Not since the night they had to flee the apartment.

The night the soldiers had come to their street in their big, military trucks, Papa had lifted Izaak from the bed in his strong arms. Together with Mama and Sarah, they had left the building by the fire escape. They'd run through dark alleys, climbed fences and run flat out until they came to Mrs. Waterman's house on the Linden Canal.

Mama and Izaak had gone into hiding in the attic in Mrs. Waterman's house.

The hiding place was too small for four people. Mrs. Waterman gave Papa and Sarah the address of another safe home in the city. Izaak wished he knew where they were. He wanted to visit them, but Mama said it was too dangerous.

Izaak listened. Footsteps sounded on the stairs. With a deep breath of relief, he recognized Mrs. Waterman's tread.

The door to the attic room opened. Izaak moved away from his mother's arms. On his knees, he waited for the dresser to slide back, so he and Mama could crawl out of their hiding place.

"It's safe now." Mrs. Waterman breathed with heavy gulps. She leaned on the dresser. Her bottom lip trembled. Her white curly hair lay damp against her forehead.

"It's too dangerous," she said. "You can't stay here any longer."

"But," Mama placed her hand over her mouth, "where will we go?"

"I don't know yet." Mrs. Waterman looked at Izaak and at Mama.

Izaak grabbed Mama's hand. He looked at her pale face.

"I don't know yet," Mrs. Waterman repeated.

# Els

Izaak and Mama were alone in the attic room.

Izaak's hands balled into fists. He stared at Mama's colorless face. "I'm not going without you, Mama!" he said.

"I know. This is hard." Mama swallowed.

Izaak's voice rose. "No, it isn't, because I'm not going!" He couldn't believe it. First, Papa and Sarah had to hide somewhere else. Now, Mama wanted to send him far away.

"It is for the best," Mama said.

"No!" Izaak stamped his feet.

"Sh." His mother grabbed his shoulders. "Sh, Izaak, we can't make noise. I don't want Mrs. Waterman to hear us. And I especially don't want the neighbors to hear us."

Izaak slumped against Mama. Tears pricked his eyes. He didn't want to cry. He was too mad.

"I don't even know these people. Where is this far away place called Friesland? And where will you go, Mama?"

"Don't worry about me, Izaak." She stroked his hair. "I will find a good hiding place too. But you will have the best place. Friesland is a province up north, a place of small villages and towns, but mainly farmland. You will go to one of the farms." Mama paused. "The farms in Friesland have enough food to feed you." Mama looked away. "There's no food left in Amsterdam. You're so skinny. You need good food while you're still growing."

His eyes caught Mama's. "How will you eat then?"

"I will be looked after, Izaak."

Anger welled up in Izaak's chest. He wanted to strike out at Hitler and his mean soldiers. He wanted to hit Mama for sending him to Friesland.

"Out in the country, the soldiers will never find you. You'll be able to go to school and play outside, instead of being cooped up in the attic day after day. There will be children for you to play with."

Mama rattled on and on. Izaak didn't want to know. He'd never been on a farm. He'd never been outside the city. The only farm animal he'd ever seen was the milkman's horse.

"You will have a new name." Mama's voice was soft now.

"A new name!" Izaak's mouth fell open. "I don't want a new name! I'm Izaak!"

"You will always be Izaak." Mama looked straight at him now. "But, in Friesland with your new family, you will be called Jan. It will only be for the time while you're there. As soon as the war is over, you can be Izaak again." Mama smiled weakly.

"Why can't we stay if the war will be over soon? You said that the southern part of the country has already been liberated."

"It will be so good for you." Mama couldn't stop talking about him going away.

"If it's so good, why aren't you coming with me?" He looked at her with dark eyes.

"It's too dangerous for me to travel. The soldiers will recognize me."

"Why isn't it dangerous for me?" Izaak persisted.

"You'll be traveling with a woman. People will think you're her child."

Izaak pulled free from his mother's grip. "I'm not going with a strange woman!" The anger bubbled up inside of him again.

"I hate this war!" he screamed.

"Izaak!" In one step, Mama caught

him. Her hand closed over his mouth. Izaak wrestled. Mama held him. Her arms wrapped around him like a vice. He kicked and struggled, but it was no use. Mama was much too strong for him.

"When am I leaving?" The tears tried to come back. He wiped his eyes with his sleeve.

"Tomorrow," Mama whispered. She took his hand. "Come, you have to help me pack. Go get your coat."

Izaak crawled into their hiding space. He dug into a cardboard box of clothing. At the bottom, he found his blue coat. He held the material against his face. It felt soft and woolen. His finger traced the yellow star that Mama had sewn on the upper left side. He hadn't worn the coat since ... Izaak didn't want to think about the night they had fled. Now, he had to flee to another hiding place. All by himself. Far away.

Izaak and Mama walked down the stairs into Mrs. Waterman's kitchen.

Mrs. Waterman sat at the table, peeling potatoes.

"They're rotten." She held up a peeled potato that looked brown.

"We'll add some more salt. They'll taste fine." Mama took Mrs. Waterman's sewing basket from a shelf behind the stove. "I'm taking the star off." Mama reached for the coat in Izaak's arms.

Izaak nodded.

Mama used tiny scissors to snip off the yellow star. "Oh, no!" She held up the coat. "Look at this. You can tell exactly where the yellow star was."

Izaak looked at his coat. A dark blue star stood out against the faded blue fabric.

"That won't do," Mrs. Waterman said. "Can you sew a pocket over top?"

Mama smiled. "Yes. I'll sew four pockets on your coat, Izaak. Two at the top and two at the bottom. You can fill them with food for your long trip."

Izaak didn't want to think about the

trip. Ever since Mama had mentioned his going away, his stomach had hurt, as if he had a ball rolling inside.

"I have some nice gray fabric." Mrs. Waterman rose from the table. She opened the pantry. "Here it is," she said. "It will be perfect." She handed Mama a piece of coarse, gray material.

"It's great." Mama winked at Izaak.

Izaak turned to face the window. He didn't want to look at his coat anymore.

Two seagulls dove into the back yard while Izaak listened to the scissors snip through the fabric.

If only that feeling in his stomach would go away. The afternoon crept by. Izaak didn't play with his horse and wagon. He watched the birds or stared at nothing in Mrs. Waterman's back yard.

Early next morning, Izaak tucked his horse and wagon in the lower right-hand pocket of his coat. His arms had grown too long for the sleeves.

He couldn't eat breakfast. The ball still filled his stomach.

Mama and Mrs. Waterman didn't speak.

Izaak looked out the kitchen window. He heard the *ding, ding* when the milkman arrived in the street.

The doorbell rang.

Mrs. Waterman left to answer it.

Izaak looked at Mama. Deep lines marked her face, from her mouth to her chin. Dark, puffy circles lay beneath her eyes.

Muffled voices floated from the hallway to the kitchen. Izaak turned towards the window. He didn't want to see the woman who was taking him so far away. He clenched his fists tight in his pockets.

"Izaak." Mrs. Waterman's voice was tight. "This is Els. She's come all the way from Friesland to take you to a safe place."

Izaak turned to look at the woman. She wore a beige raincoat. A flowered scarf was tied around her chin. A few blond curls escaped from the scarf and framed her face. Els didn't look like a woman, Izaak thought. She looked like a big girl.

"How old are you?" Mama asked.

The girl's face turned bright red. "Eighteen," she answered.

"Aren't you too young to ... ," Mama's voice ended in a whisper.

"I've taken many children safely to Friesland," Els said.

Izaak couldn't speak. He looked from Mama to the girl. The kitchen turned silent.

"Here. Your coat. Put it on." Mama hurried his arms into the sleeves. She reached for the bag with his clothing. Izaak felt like a rag doll. He couldn't button up his coat. His legs wouldn't move. He felt Mama's wet cheek when she kissed him good-bye. The front door opened. Els took her bicycle. She tucked his bag into the saddlebags.

Izaak straddled the carrier at the

back of the bike, his feet resting inside the saddlebags.

Els mounted the bike. Izaak looked at Els's back. He held onto her coat. He couldn't see ahead. The front door of Mrs. Waterman's house closed with a click. Tall thin houses passed by on one side and the canal passed by on the other.

# The Long Trip

October winds brushed Izaak's cheeks and ruffled his hair like leaves in the wind. His hands gripped the cloth of Els's raincoat. Military trucks blared their horns. Izaak cringed at the *ding, ding* of the streetcar and the squealing of brakes. Behind him people shouted. Izaak had never seen so many people. Some pushed wheelbarrows, baby carriages and wooden wagons. Children cried, their faces smudged.

"Watch out!" a woman yelled.

The bike swerved. Izaak struggled to stay put.

"Don't move, Jan!" Els shouted over her shoulder.

Jan! She called him Jan! Izaak tightened his grip on the coat. He clenched his jaw and looked down at Els's feet turning the pedals round and round. The bricks in the street whizzed past until he got dizzy and had to look up.

Els turned left over a bridge. Once they were over the top of the bridge, they coasted downhill fast. Els didn't even have to move her feet. She rang the bell, and people jumped out of the way. The wind stroked Izaak's face. A group of soldiers marched ahead of them, singing. Left, right, left, right, their feet matched the beat of the marching song. Izaak glanced sideways at them. Els passed so close, Izaak could see the stubble on their chins. His heart pounded. The ball in his stomach squeezed and rolled.

They turned again and crossed more bridges until they left the busy streets of the city behind.

Soon after that, Els halted. "Would you like to stretch your legs?" she asked breathlessly.

Izaak nodded. His words were still stuck. He felt like crying, but he wouldn't.

"We have a long way to ride." Els looked at him. Her eyes were bright blue and friendly.

"By eight o'clock tonight, we need to get to the farm where we'll sleep. We'll stop once to eat."

Izaak looked at her. He didn't feel hungry. He didn't care about food. He didn't want to stay overnight. He wanted to go back to the attic in Mrs. Waterman's house. He wanted to go back to Mama.

"We might get stopped by the soldiers at checkpoints."

Izaak's eyes widened. Weren't they safe now that they were out of the big city?

"When they stop us and ask questions, don't say a word. Just look at your shoes. I will do all the talking. Understood?" Her voice was stern.

Izaak could only nod. As long as his voice was stuck, he couldn't speak to anyone.

"Let's go."

Izaak climbed back on the carrier. Els mounted the bike. Izaak watched the landscape change. They passed clumps of houses and meadows dotted with grazing black and white cows. Clouds of leaves blew across farmers' fields as Els and Izaak rode between villages and towns.

Much later, Els dismounted again in front of a bakery. The smell of freshly baked bread greeted them, but it made the ball in Izaak's stomach turn.

After she leaned the bike against the wall of the store, Els pushed him ahead. The *cling-clang* of the little bell above the door announced their entrance. A woman with a smiling red face and a boxlike body stood behind the counter. The sleeves of her shirt were rolled up and her arms were covered in white flour.

She talked loudly to Els while her dentures rattled. Izaak couldn't understand a word she said. Els nudged him.

"Jan, Mrs. de Beer asked if you wanted a bun."

Izaak nodded. He had no idea how he was going to add a bun to the ball in his stomach.

"Here." Els handed him one. It was still warm.

Izaak nodded at the woman and tucked the bun in his pocket with the metal horse.

"Thank you." Els ushered him out of the store and onto the bike.

Izaak's bottom hurt from bouncing on the hard, metal carrier. They wouldn't get to the farm for a long time. Els didn't talk to him anymore. She strained forward against the wind.

Once more she dismounted.

She looked at him. "Do you need to pee?"

Izaak nodded and disappeared behind a tree.

"We're going for the last stretch," she said after he'd climbed back on his seat. "We have to hurry to get there before eight."

Izaak nodded again. He knew that was called curfew. After eight o'clock the Germans didn't allow anyone to be out on the street.

The trip seemed to take forever. Izaak tried not to think. He rested his head against Els's back and looked sideways. Cold and numb, he watched black crows sitting on a fence. Ducks made smooth landings on the water, and hundreds of seagulls swooped down on a newly plowed field. He watched until his eyelids drooped and his head sagged.

A loud rumbling sound startled Izaak awake. He almost lost his balance. The bike swerved. He grabbed Els's coat. It took him a second to realize that the roar came from the sky.

Els stopped and let him stretch his legs. Izaak looked up. He squeezed his eyes and made out a formation of planes.

"They're going to Germany," Els said. "They're going to drop bombs to make Germany stop the war."

Good, Izaak thought. From the attic window, he'd often seen the white trails crisscrossing the sky. He'd trailed the patterns with his finger until the lines faded away. He wished hundreds, no, millions of planes would drop bombs on Germany. As soon as the war stopped, he could go back to his family. Tears threatened again when he thought of his parents.

"Time to go, Jan. We have two hours left to get to the farm. One hour left till curfew."

Izaak climbed on the bike. Two hours seemed like a long time. He didn't feel so good. His head was light and the ball rolled and rolled in his stomach. He didn't watch the landscape anymore. Dusk settled over the fields. He leaned his head against Els and closed his eyes.

The bike skidded to a halt. Izaak slid to one side. As Els jumped off, Izaak fell from the bike onto the stone-paved road. He wrapped his arms around his head and rolled onto his side. A sharp pain shot through his hip. At the same time, a rumbling sound grew louder. He opened his eyes. Darkness surrounded him. Els had disappeared. Panic flooded his chest. He cried out.

In the next moment, Els jumped up from the slope of the canal and screamed at him, "Jan! We have to hide! A truck! Soldiers!"

Izaak tried to get up, but his legs didn't work, just like in a nightmare he'd had once. A huge wolf had been chasing him. He had wanted to run, but his legs wouldn't move. As the wolf pounced on him, Papa had been there to comfort him. Now the wolf had turned into a military truck full of soldiers and Papa was far away.

"Jan! Move!" Els screamed. "The

soldiers must not find us! We have to hide! They'll kill us! It's past curfew!"

Izaak jumped to his feet fast as a cannonball. He grabbed Els's hand and she pulled him down the slope of the canal that ran alongside the road. As he slid down, he noticed the bicycle down in the reeds.

"Stay flat on your stomach!" Els yelled in his ear. "Keep your head down!"

Izaak tried to follow her instructions as the rumbling came closer. His heart pounded in his ears. He heard Els's loud breathing beside him. She'd put her arm around his shoulder. They lay still, just like Izaak and Mama in the hiding place, both afraid to breathe when the soldiers searched the attic.

The earth trembled when the military truck passed by.

Izaak did not move. Exhaust fumes filled his nostrils. Finally, Els raised her head. She looked both ways. She pulled Izaak to his feet, found her bike and dragged it back up the slope. Izaak followed. The hand in his pocket squished past the bun until he felt the metal horse.

"That was close," Els panted. "We're almost there."

Dazed, Izaak mounted again and off they went. Darkness followed them, and the tall outlines of trees crept closer and closer. Finally, Els turned into a lane with tall trees on either side.

That night, Els and Izaak slept in the soft hay of the barn of a strange farm. Early next morning, before the farmer was up, they continued their trip north to Friesland.

# The New Family

"He doesn't talk and he doesn't eat."

Els pushed Izaak ahead of her into the farm kitchen. She took off her raincoat.

All day, Els had ridden hard and Izaak had sat dazed and confused on the carrier. Long past curfew, they had entered the lane to a large farm. The farm buildings loomed ahead of them. Izaak had arrived at his new home. The ball in his stomach was bigger than ever.

A large woman, her hands on her hips, looked at Izaak. Izaak looked at

the floor. The next moment he was ·
squashed in an enormous hug.

"Oh, you skinny minny," the woman
sang. "No wonder you don't talk and
can't eat. Look what's happened to you.
You're far away from your parents. You
don't even know where they are. A strange
girl comes, plops you on her bike and
takes you all the way to Friesland to a
farm with people you've never seen before."

She pushed Izaak into a big arm-
chair close to the window and ruffled
his hair. "I'm Aunt Anna," she said,
"and you are Jan de Vries, our nephew
from Amsterdam. Welcome to our farm."
Izaak looked at her face. Her eyes sparkled. Strands of gray curly hair had
escaped from a bun at the back of her
head. She wore a checkered apron over
a flowery dress and she smelled of
warmth, animals and food.

"Tomorrow you'll meet all the animals and the people who live and work
at the farm. Last night we brought
the horses inside for the winter."

Horses. That was the last thought that crossed Izaak's mind before his head touched the armrest of the chair.

Izaak awoke to the chirping of birds. He reached beside him, expecting to find Mama. Then he remembered.

Light footsteps made their way to his door. They stopped. Izaak held his breath.

The door opened. Izaak sat up.

"Sun is shining. The cows are up!" a girl's voice sang. She bounced into the room and pulled up the blackout curtains. Sunlight poured in. Izaak looked around. The single bed he'd slept in stood against the wall. A large dresser and a chair stood against the opposite wall. Two tall windows let the sun in. He looked at the girl. She stood at the window and stared at him. The sun lit her long wavy hair with fire. Freckles were splashed all over her face. Her eyes, big and oval, questioned him.

"I'm Annie. You're Jan and you're eight," she sang.

"Eight-and-a-half." Izaak was startled by his own voice.

"Els said you didn't speak." She marched to the door and left the room.

Els. Izaak remembered. Did she live on the farm too?

"Wait!" Izaak called. He jumped out of bed and ran out the door. He still wore his clothes from yesterday. He stood in the doorway and listened. Which way to go now?

"The cows are eating breakfast."

Annie's high voice guided him along the hallway, down seven steps and another hallway till he walked into a brightly lit kitchen. He vaguely remembered the room from last night. Voices, low and deep, smells of food, the banging of cutlery overwhelmed him. He stopped in the doorway.

"So, this is Jan." A deep voice drew Izaak's eyes to a man with a shiny bald head, sitting at the head of a large rectangular table. Sharp cheekbones carved his face. Dark eyes looked at Izaak. Izaak's heart beat fast.

"Uncle Piet." Annie climbed on the man's lap and patted his head.

"We need to put Jan out to pasture with the cows, Annie," Uncle Piet said. "He's skin and bone and white as milk."

Izaak didn't know what "out to pasture" meant.

"Oh, he's just kidding." The woman whom he had met last night, Aunt Anna, took his hand and led him to the table.

They passed a large wicker basket beside the black stove. A long-haired dog with black and white patches lifted its head. A calico cat and a black cat with white paws were curled up beside the dog. Izaak wasn't used to animals. His family had never owned a cat or a dog.

"The dog's name is Bijke." Annie hopped from Uncle Piet's lap and crouched down beside the basket. "The black cat is Moorke." She lifted the calico cat in her arms. "This is my favorite. I named her Princess."

Izaak tried to take it all in, but Aunt Anna pulled him away from the basket.

Looking around the large table, he saw Els. She smiled at him. Slouched in a chair beside her sat a boy much older than Izaak. His hair hung over his eyes. The skin on one side of his face was a deep reddish purple. Izaak's stomach tightened. The boy didn't look up.

Annie pointed at the boy. "That's Gabe," she said. "Gabe doesn't talk much either, but his birthday is coming up soon. He's going to be sixteen. And this is Albert Adema." Annie pointed to the person beside Gabe. "He lives in the house beside the farm and has lots of children."

A smile lit up the man's face. "Hi, Jan. The more children, the merrier. My son Jaap is the same age as you."

Izaak didn't know what to say or

where to look. He wasn't used to so many people.

"All right, Annie." Aunt Anna carried steaming plates to the table. "Make some room for Jan. And you have to eat quickly or you'll be late for school."

Izaak slid into a spot between Annie and Albert.

"Is Jan coming to school with me?" Annie shoved a spoonful of food into her mouth.

"Not yet." Aunt Anna placed a flat bowl in front of him. "He has to get used to the farm and the people first."

"And he needs some meat on his bones," Uncle Piet added, "or the wind will blow him over."

Izaak looked at the table. A basket was filled with thick slices of dark rye bread. Tall glasses of milk stood at each place. A chunk of cheese as big and round as a wheel was ready for slicing. And wheat porridge steamed in Izaak's bowl. He hadn't seen that much food since ... He stirred the porridge in his bowl and took a small spoonful. It was warm and sweet. He was glad Aunt Anna had only given him a little bit. His stomach felt so full. The ball was still there. While Izaak ate, cutlery clattered and voices hummed in the warm kitchen.

"Do you think the Allied troops will get here before the winter?" Albert moved his finger around his bowl in a circle and licked it.

"The Germans seem to have a stronghold at the rivers," Uncle Piet answered in a deep voice. "As long as the Allied armies can't cross the rivers, we will be at war."

Chairs scraped on the wooden floor, and the men got up. They took their caps from a row of hooks on the wall beside a wooden door and left, followed by Bijke, the dog. Els got up too. She ruffled Izaak's hair. "I know you will have a good safe place here." Els took her raincoat off the hook and was off.

"Where is Els going?" Izaak looked at the closed door.

"We don't know," Aunt Anna said. "She is always on a secret mission."

Els was brave, Izaak thought. She could have been caught by the soldiers on the way to Friesland with him.

Izaak's eyes followed Annie as she hopped around the kitchen, petting the cats.

"Here." Aunt Anna held out a red coat. "Skedaddle!"

Annie smiled at Izaak as she went out.

"As soon as Nel comes, we'll get the bathtub ready." Aunt Anna said. "After, I'll take you to the stables and the barn. You're safe here, Jan. The soldiers won't find you." She carried the plates and cups to the sink. A large, black kettle on the stove blew ringlets of steam. Izaak watched them curl up.

"Have you been on a farm before?"

Izaak shook his head. His throat

closed. How he wished he was back in the attic with Mama and Mrs. Waterman.

"Now, now." Aunt Anna stood beside him and stroked his hair. Her arm tightened around his shoulders. She held him just like Mama, but she smelled of wood and farm and Mama smelled like ...

The door opened and closed.

"Good morning, Nel." Aunt Anna greeted a tall woman with strawberry-blond hair.

"Good morning." The woman hung her coat on a hook. She shivered. "It's a good day to stay close to the stove," she said. "This must be Jan."

"This is Nel." Aunt Anna said. "She's Albert's wife. She helps out every morning. Can you get the basin, Nel? Jan needs a little soaking."

Nel disappeared again and returned a minute later with a galvanized tub. She placed it in front of the stove. Aunt Anna filled the tub with the water from the kettle. Nel added a bucket of cold water.

Izaak shivered. He couldn't remember the last time he'd taken a bath. Mrs. Waterman had thought it too dangerous.

"I brought some clothes that Jaap has outgrown, but they'll be too large for Jan." Nel hung a pair of brown pants and a checkered shirt over the back of a chair and left the kitchen.

Aunt Anna handed him a washcloth, a towel and a bar of soap. Then she left the kitchen as well.

Izaak looked around. The cats slept in the dog basket. The grandfather clock ticked.

He took off his clothes and climbed into the tub. The warm water hugged his shivering body.

# Hero

"Here, Bijke!" Aunt Anna patted the dog. "Say hello to Jan, you lazy dog."

The dog wagged its tail. Hesitantly, Izaak placed his hand on the dog's head. Bijke sniffed his pants. The dog's tongue reached up to lick Izaak's arm, then his hand. The soft wet tongue tickled his skin. Izaak laughed.

Aunt Anna took his hand. "We'll meet the calves next." Together they walked the length of the barn past farm equipment. Izaak looked up at the high beams and piles of hay in the loft. Bijke followed closely.

Izaak's nostrils filled with the smell of hay, manure and animals.

Aunt Anna opened a door and they entered another part of the barn. Light shone in through two square windows and fanned out through the openings of the gate, leaving a striped pattern on the straw.

When he looked through the bars of a gate, Izaak discovered black and white calves. The floor was covered with a thick layer of yellow straw. Three calves were lying down, but most of them were gathered around a trough filled with milk. One calf with a black face was pushing aside two others, to get closer to the trough. Another calf stared at the visitors, his eyes large and questioning.

"There should be fourteen," Aunt Anna said.

Izaak counted. A little one came to the gate and Aunt Anna let it suck on her fingers. "This one was born yesterday," she said. "They love sucking my fingers, because they have to learn to drink from a bucket as soon as they're born. They miss suckling their mother. Here, climb up." She pulled her hand free and helped him up to the top of the gate. "Now, you're the king of the farm." Her laugh bubbled around him.

From behind the next door, Izaak heard voices and the clanging of metal.

"Come." Aunt Anna reached for his hand and Izaak jumped down. "The men are cleaning out the manure and fixing up the straw underneath the cows." She opened the door. A wave of warmth touched Izaak's face and a much stronger smell of manure engulfed him.

His mouth opened as he stood in the doorway. Black and white bodies lined both sides of the stable. A wide path covered with yellow straw ran down the middle. Uncle Piet and Albert were using pitchforks to straighten and fluff the straw underneath each cow. Gabe was scooping manure into a wheelbarrow that was filled almost to the top.

"Gabe!" Uncle Piet called. "Leave the manure for Albert. Take Jan to Hero. The sooner he gets to know him, the better."

Gabe looked up. He left the wheelbarrow, wiped his hands on his coveralls and motioned for Izaak to follow.

Izaak held back, but a nod from Aunt Anna encouraged him.

Gabe was silent as Izaak walked behind him through a wooden door.

As soon as the door opened, Izaak heard the horses. Three enclosures housed gleaming, black animals. They were not at all like Bessie from the milk wagon. These horses' coats were a deep black. Long manes covered their eyes. The muscles in their bodies bulged.

One at the time, Gabe patted the horses' flanks.

Now that he had come close, Izaak noticed their strong bodies. All three turned their heads to watch him. While Gabe checked their feed in a long trough made of metal bars that ran the full length of the wall, the horses watched Izaak from beneath their black manes. Their eyes shone dark and proud. The one closest to him was the tallest and most muscular.

Gabe moved his hand down the tall horse's back and, for the first time that day, looked at Izaak. Izaak shivered when he looked at Gabe's purple face. It reminded him of a picture of a two-headed monster he'd seen in a book a long time ago. The monster's heads had been swollen and purple too.

"Come," Gabe reached for his hand. "Stroke his side so he knows you're here."

Izaak touched the horse's coat. It felt warm and coarse and smooth all at the same time.

Strong arms lifted Izaak close to the animal's head.

"This is Hero," Gabe said. Izaak heard pride in his voice. "He is a famous stallion. You and Hero have something in common,

Jan. You are both wanted by the Germans."

Izaak gasped.

"Don't worry. They are never going to get either of you. Trust me. That's why I want you to make friends with Hero."

Izaak didn't understand.

"Move your hands through his mane." Gabe still held him up and, with his hand covering Izaak's, they stroked the horse's mane and head.

A sudden calm came over Izaak. The feel of the warm body and Gabe's arm comforted him.

"Whenever the Germans come and search the farm, you have to climb into the trough without startling the horses. Always talk to them and stroke their bodies before you walk into the enclosure beside them. Climb into the trough, cover yourself with hay, and lie as still as possible." Gabe set Izaak down. Now he stood beside the tall stallion. He looked at the legs that were covered with long hair as well, as if Hero were wearing fur-covered boots.

"This is Marijke," Gabe stroked the nose and ruffled the mane of the horse beside Hero.

"She's our best mare. In the spring she'll have a foal. Beside Marijke is Clasina, Hero's mother. Clasina is a little skittish, especially if she doesn't know you."

Gabe seemed to know everything about the horses. Izaak wished he knew about horses too. He stood close to Hero's face and smelled the strong smell of the animal. Hero's nostrils trembled. He gazed calmly at Izaak. Izaak's heart skipped. Without thinking, he touched the smooth skin of Hero's face. Hero nuzzled his sleeve. Izaak smiled. His cheeks burned. He felt like he was in a magical dream.

"See," Gabe murmured. "Hero wants to make friends already."

For a moment Izaak had forgotten about the boy with the purple face.

Now he looked at him again; Gabe didn't look like a monster at all.

"Twice a day, before and after school, you will help take care of the horses."

Izaak walked past Hero, remembering to stroke the horse while he walked beside him. A warm feeling filled his chest, the first good feeling he had had since he'd left Amsterdam.

# School

"Jan, I'm not waiting!" Annie's voice sang out.

Izaak buttoned the green, rubber coat and pulled the hood over his head. He stuffed his feet into wooden clogs and followed Annie out the door. Together they ran down the lane to the house near the farm. Raindrops pelted them like small stones. As he skipped to avoid one puddle, he landed in another. The water splashed over his clogs, soaking his socks. He laughed, stretched his arms and held up the palms of his hands. The water tickled his fingers.

He licked the rain from his lips. He sprinted to catch up with Annie. Her hood had come off and her red curly hair bounced up and down in stretched ringlets.

Annie had been at the farm much longer than he had. She was Jewish just like him. The only difference was that Annie didn't look Jewish.

Annie's cries sang in the early November morning. He couldn't keep up with her. She headed for the small house at the end of the farm buildings. Albert, Nel and their six children filled the small but tidy dwelling.

From behind the bare wooden door appeared Harm, a tall boy, wearing a black cap and Elizabeth, his sister, with long, spindly legs. Next came Jaap, a boy Izaak's age, followed by the twins, Klaas and Durk, who were six. One older girl, Mien, worked in the village at the bakery.

For the last month, Izaak had joined this group of children as they walked the one-and-a-half kilometer road to the village. They all attended the two-room school. Jaap and Izaak were in grade three, the twins and Annie in grade one. The headmaster, Mr. Abma, taught Elizabeth in grade five and Harm in grade six.

Izaak, Jaap, Annie and the twins had a teacher named Miss Afke.

While they tromped and splashed through puddles and mud, Izaak thought about school. Since the war began, he hadn't been allowed at school. Jews were forbidden to go anywhere. They couldn't walk in parks, go on buses and streetcars or in many stores. He was glad he could go to school here. Life on the farm kept him busy as well. Every morning before school, he fed Hero and made sure the stallion had enough fresh straw for the day while Gabe looked after the other two horses. Hero greeted Izaak as soon as he opened the door to the stable. Izaak's chest filled with warmth every time he stroked

Hero's neck and ruffled the long thick mane.

On the first day of school, the children of the village had stared at him. A big boy with a mean smile had called him a "dirty Jew" and had pushed him during recess. Izaak froze, but Harm and Jaap had been right there, so the boy had sulked away. From that day on Izaak felt safe with Albert and Nel's children. They were rough and loud, especially the twins, but he liked them.

After school, they often came over to the farm. They played hide-and-go-seek. The farm was isolated. It was built on a man-made hill called a terp. A wide moat girded the farm buildings. Sometimes, Jaap and Izaak walked through the fields with Bijke. Jaap knew the names of all the meadow birds. They climbed the dike and walked along the top.

"Not the sea dike that protects the land from the sea," Jaap explained, "but the one before that."

Standing on top of the dike, Izaak could see the real dike in the distance. Farm buildings lay scattered between the two dikes. He stretched his arms as if he wanted to embrace the land and the sky. The land was so flat that he could see many villages and towns in the distance. To the southwest he saw steeples, factory chimneys and the windmill that used to grind the wheat for the town of Dokkum.

When he'd first arrived on the farm, he'd often thought about Mama, Papa and Sarah. When he closed his eyes tightly, he could see Mama's tired face and Sarah's big smile. He remembered Papa's voice, but lately he had trouble picturing his father's features. Being outside all day, Izaak was so exhausted that he fell asleep right away. The ball in his tummy had disappeared and he tried to eat as much as Gabe. Aunt Anna was pleased when he ate so much. She said Gabe had two hollow legs and that's why Izaak couldn't keep up with him yet.

"Hey, Jan!" Jaap waited for him. "How come you're falling behind?"

Izaak caught up with Jaap.

"I hope Miss Afke will read to us today." Jaap's face was dripping with rain.

"I hope she will too."

Every Saturday morning for the last half hour, Miss Afke read to her students. The book she was reading to them now was about a horse. A horse as black and strong as Hero, named Sytse. Her voice carried Izaak far away. He imagined he was the boy riding the horse, galloping along the shore of the North Sea, the wind in his hair, sand spraying every time hooves hit the beach. The story made Izaak forget about the war, about Mama, Papa, Sarah and the German soldiers. The story of the black stallion reminded Izaak of Hero. He shivered as he thought of the powerful animal with his strong, muscled body and deep, black color. One day soon he would ride Hero. Gabe had promised. Izaak couldn't wait.

Ahead of them, the twins tumbled over each other and landed in a big puddle.

"Hey! Break it up!" Harm grabbed the two rascals by their coat collars and pulled them apart.

Since Izaak had started attending the small village school, two more children had arrived. A girl with long, black braids and a shy smile had come two weeks after him. Last week, a skinny, pale-faced boy had started grade one. He cried often and the big children made fun of him.

They neared the village square where the church stood high and proud. Just past the church and the cemetery stood the small brick school. At exactly eight o'clock, they all tumbled inside.

Despite the damp weather, their classroom was warm. One by one the children hung their wet clothes on a drying rack that stood around a black potbellied wood stove near the back of the classroom.

"Find your seats." Over her ebony-rimmed glasses, Miss Afke made sure that everyone's coat had a chance to dry.

The children filed to their desks, according to their grade level. Izaak sat behind Jaap, five rows from the back of the room. One side of the classroom had large windows, but the windowsills were so high that the students could only look out when they were standing up.

"Grade threes, we'll start with math this morning. Look at the blackboard. All your questions are there." Miss Afke watched as the noise level diminished and the students looked for their fountain pens.

"I have received some paper from the hospital." Miss Afke handed out square pieces of yellow paper. "Please work neatly. Next week we'll have to work on slates again."

Izaak smoothed the yellow paper and smelled its hospital scent. On one side were black numbers. Perhaps between the numbers and the margins he could draw small animals.

Jaap turned around. "Wouldn't it be neat if we had x-rays on one side?"

The sharp voice of their teacher turned Jaap back to his work.

The class fell silent except for the scratching sounds of the fountain pens on the x-ray paper. Izaak didn't have trouble with math even though he had never attended school. Mama had taught him that subject as well as reading to fill the time in the attic. As soon as Miss Afke explained the math questions, he got excited. He worked fast. When he finished his assignment, he started drawing a black stallion with a long mane, a powerful body and a proud head. Izaak dreamed of riding Hero.

The loud scream of sirens startled everybody out of their desks. Air Raid!

Once in a while they heard the alarm at night, when the planes came close to the farm, the whole family stumbled out of bed into a shelter in the hay barn. Allied planes flying east sometimes dropped their bombs before they reached Germany. Or a stray bomb could fall from a plane that had been attacked by anti-aircraft fire.

"Everyone underneath the window-sill." Miss Afke scrambled with the students to the safety of the wall. Most grade ones cried, except for Klaas and Durk. Students climbed over each other in order to find a spot. Legs and arms got twisted, resulting in screams.

"We must stay calm." Miss Afke shouted over the wailing alarm and the crying children.

Jaap squished between Izaak and a stocky boy named Wim. "I don't think we'd be safe if a bomb smacked into the school," he said.

"Quiet. We might hear the planes." Miss Afke tried again. But as long as the alarm howled, they could hear nothing else.

Izaak watched Annie, who sat nearby.

She wound her arms around her knees, closed her eyes and rocked. Before going to sleep each night, Annie cried for her mother and rocked. She rocked until Aunt Anna unwound her arms and covered her with the blanket.

Izaak closed his eyes. The ball in his stomach was back and he felt like he had to throw up. With his hand pressed hard against his mouth and his arm holding his stomach, he waited. Waited for the noise to stop, for the screaming to subside.

An enormous boom shook the building, followed by the shattering of glass. The walls trembled, shards of glass fell like hailstones, smashing when they hit the floor.

With his head between his knees, Izaak tried to block out all the noise. He was sure that he was going to die now. The building was going to collapse and then it wouldn't matter that they were all sitting under the windowsill.

The other children had moved away from the wall.

Jaap tapped his shoulder. "Jan! It's over!"

Slowly, Izaak lifted his head. The room was quiet. The students were silent. Even Miss Afke stood still and looked with big eyes at the chaos of broken glass. The force of the blast had scattered glass all over the room.

When she finally spoke, Miss Afke's voice trembled. "Don't touch a thing. I want you to get your coats and clogs. Shake the glass off and go home."

They did as they were told. Izaak and Jaap stood outside in the playground and waited for the others.

The small group walked home in silence.

Later, they learned that an Allied plane had dropped a stray bomb just outside the village, before it had crashed into the Wadden Sea. The bomb had destroyed a house and killed a mother and her child.

# Skating

That stray bomb left the school building without windows. Once the openings were boarded up, the two classrooms turned into dark spooky places. The days grew shorter and the weather turned cold. The children still went to school, but they now had to keep their coats on because of a shortage of wood for the small stove. Sometimes when Miss Afke read to them, she lit a candle. They huddled around her.

December reminded Izaak of the celebration of light, Chanukah. He thought of his family and how for eight nights they had lit their menorah, adding one candle every night. Last year, when his family had been apart and in hiding they hadn't celebrated Chanukah. And this year ... Tears filled his eyes; he didn't even know where his family was.

As the temperature dipped below freezing, Izaak found that the best place to be was with the animals in the stables. Their bodies gave off enough heat to keep him warm.

One morning the windows in the bedroom were covered with a thick layer of frost. Izaak and Annie blew holes in the frozen patterns with their warm breath.

"Soon we will go skating," Annie said.

Izaak looked at her. "I don't know how," he said. "I don't have skates."

"You will get hand-me-downs from the children next door."

He'd never skated before, but the thought filled him with excitement.

The school closed. The temperature

dropped further. The Germans cut off the electricity.

The ice on the moat shone like glass, the sky was a clear winter's blue and the wind blew calm from the east.

When the layer of ice on the moat that surrounded the farm was strong enough, the children all came with their skates.

Albert and Nel brought a box filled with wooden skates. Izaak and Annie had to try on several pairs before they found some that were the right length for their feet. They tied the skates to their sturdy, leather, laced-up boots.

Gabe helped Izaak tie his skates. "Watch closely," Gabe said. "I'm only showing you once."

Izaak nodded. As soon as Gabe pulled him up from the embankment, Izaak's feet slid everywhere, and before he could even think how to work his legs he fell flat on his back on the ice.

They all cheered and heat rose in Izaak's cheeks.

"I'll get you a chair." Aunt Anna rushed inside. Izaak waited until she came back with a wooden chair.

"That's how I learned last year." Annie wobbled dangerously close to Izaak, but kept her balance.

As soon as Aunt Anna placed the chair in front of him, Izaak felt more secure. He pushed it and kept his balance as the skates went left, right, left, right on the shiny ice.

Gabe laughed as he passed him in long, even strides. "Keep your tongue in your mouth, Jan," he said. "It might get frostbite."

Izaak watched Gabe. Oh, if he could skate like him one day. Left, right, left, right. He pushed himself along. Annie and the twins passed him too, but Izaak kept going. And in the next few days, Izaak's practicing paid off. He left the chair at the bank, and although he still wobbled, he managed to improve.

At night he slept like a bale of hay, exhausted from the outdoor exercise.

The children skated for a whole week until a thaw set in and ruined the ice.

But winter wasn't over yet. January brought extreme cold and more ice and snow.

"We'll get the sleigh ready," Uncle Piet announced one morning. "I think Hero would like some winter fun too."

"Hero?" Izaak's eyes grew larger.

"Yes." Uncle Piet smiled. "Aunt Anna and Nel will polish the harness bells and Albert and Gabe will clean out the sleigh. This afternoon we'll take Hero out."

Izaak dug deep into his porridge. He couldn't wait.

"You're going to pull the sleigh," Izaak told Hero as he brushed the stallion's winter coat until it gleamed a deep black. At the same time, Albert hammered special nails in the horse's hooves. The horses had been outside to exercise, but never on the ice.

"We don't want Hero to slip and break something," Albert explained. "The nails don't hurt because the hoof is like your fingernails."

Izaak had thought it must be something like that. He knew these people would never do anything to hurt their animals.

After the noon meal, the whole family watched as Uncle Piet harnessed Hero. Hero's nostrils flared. His ears wiggled. He neighed over and over again. He was anxious to go outside and stretch his legs.

Izaak had never seen such a beautiful sleigh. The wood was carved at the front. The driver straddled at the back and there was a little bench in the middle for one passenger. The sleigh was painted a dark red with gold trim along the edges. The steel runners gleamed.

Gabe held onto Hero while Uncle Piet and Albert pushed the sleigh outside. Carefully, the men slid the sleigh onto the ice. Gabe followed, leading Hero. Once they had hitched the sleigh to the harness, Uncle Piet barely had time to grab the reins before the powerful stallion took off.

Izaak couldn't believe his eyes. This was like a fairy tale.

Everyone applauded when Uncle Piet passed by. Hero had taken him all around the farm buildings and back in a flash.

Uncle Piet let the stallion run for a while until he'd spent some of his energy.

Then he halted in front of the small gathering. "Come on, Anna," he said. Aunt Anna, her biggest smile on her face, sat down on the little wooden bench and off they went. The sleigh slid light as a feather across the surface. Hero didn't have to pull. He just ran. The mane flew to one side and the bells clanged. Izaak clapped his hands, watching the scene.

Everyone got a turn to ride with Uncle Piet. Finally it was Izaak's turn. He climbed up onto the small bench. His face glowed; his eyes sparkled. "Go Hero!" he called.

"You will guide him next, Jan," Uncle Piet said as snow-covered pastures flew by on one side and barns and stables flew by on the other.

Hero trotted gracefully. His ears twitched. Steam rose from his warm body.

"Now, you hold the reins." Uncle Piet moved aside, so that Izaak could sit on the wooden bar at the back of the sleigh. "Here are the brakes," Uncle Piet explained. "You press your feet down on the pedals and pull on the reins when you want the sleigh to slow down."

Izaak could feel the blood rushing through his veins.

Uncle Piet walked beside the sleigh. "Start slowly," he said. "Jaap, come sit on the bench."

Jaap smiled at Izaak before he sat down. "Way to go, Jan," he said.

Izaak beamed. He would never get enough of this. The afternoon went by in a flash.

That night, he thought about the sleighing event over and over again. In his mind he saw Hero's powerful muscles as the great horse trotted before the sleigh. For the first time since he had been at the farm, Izaak forgot to think of Mama, Papa and Sarah.

# The Courier

At the end of February the weather turned milder, and school began again.

One morning, a young woman walked into their classroom. The students' eyes followed her as she walked up to Miss Afke and whispered in her ear. Miss Afke nodded. The woman turned and walked out the door. All eyes were on the teacher. They all knew the woman was a messenger, a courier.

One by one, Miss Afke stopped at the desks of the "new" children. "Jan," she whispered, standing beside him, her hand touching his shoulder. "You need to go home. There is a roundup of people."

Izaak gasped. He looked at his teacher, his eyes large.

"And cattle and horses," she added.

He couldn't move.

Gently, Miss Afke pulled him out of his desk and guided him to the coats.

Izaak looked around. Jaap was staring at him, his face creased in an angry scowl.

Izaak's eyes went to Annie. Her eyes were big and round. Her face shone pale against the red of her hair. She knew. She was only six, but she knew what was going on. Even though she was Jewish, everybody counted on the Germans never suspecting her because of her red hair.

Izaak left the building with several other children, but soon found himself alone on the long stretch home. Fear gripped him. As he jogged along, Izaak realized this was the first time he had gone home alone.

He took a big gulp of air and started to run. He didn't look back. He ran out of the village, down the lane to the farm.

They're going to find me, he thought. If I don't hurry, they will find me.

A memory flashed through his head, a memory of German trucks rumbling down his street, a memory of him and Mama and Papa and Sarah climbing fences, hiding behind buildings before dashing across to the next street.

His clogs moved fast on the dirt road until his legs ached. A stitch in his side slowed him down. He looked behind him. No one was following him. There were no military trucks on the road.

A thought popped into his mind. He was not the only one in danger. Gabe. Gabe was in danger too. He must warn him.

And Hero. Hero was also wanted by the Germans. They must hide Hero. Where could they hide the stallion?

As his feet picked up speed, his brain searched for a hiding place for Hero. Where could they hide a big horse like Hero?

Izaak slipped in a puddle and lost one of his clogs. He bent to pick it up, took his other one off and ran in socked feet until he reached the barn. The door opened. Gasping for breath, Izaak fell inside. Two arms caught him.

"Hey!" Gabe cried out. "You scared me half to death."

Izaak looked up into Gabe's face. He saw Gabe's eyes. In the dimly lit barn, Gabe's eyes shone a soft brown. They were filled with concern.

"There's a roundup." Izaak wriggled free. "We have to hide Hero," he said. "I have been thinking."

"You know your hiding place in Hero's trough." Gabe walked toward the horse stables. Izaak followed right behind.

"But where are we going to hide him?" Izaak asked.

Gabe turned to look at him. "It's

too late to take him to the blacksmith in the village."

"We'll find something here," Izaak said. "We'll take him out in the barn where the hay used to be and cover him."

The soft glow in Gabe's eyes was gone. "That won't work, Jan," he said. "You go into your hiding spot now." His voice rose. "We can't save Hero!"

Izaak stepped into the stable beside Hero. He stroked the stallion's neck. "I will save you, Hero. I will," he said.

Gabe stood beside him, ready to lift him into the feeding trough.

"The dike!" Izaak screamed. "Why don't we take him behind the sea dike. We will be hidden too!"

Gabe's mouth opened. "Let's not lose any time."

Gabe untied Hero and led the horse out into the hay barn. "Go outside and look for military trucks. If you don't see them let's try the dike."

Izaak hurried to the door. He looked down the farm lane.

"It's clear," he shouted and opened the door wide.

Gabe had harnessed the horse with a bridle and a short rein. "Come here," he said. "I'll give you a lift."

Izaak stood close to Hero. The horse trotted on the spot. Izaak felt the tension in the animal's body build as he mounted.

"Hold on to the mane." Gabe walked the horse outside. They stood for a moment and listened. Straining their ears, they heard the low rumbling of trucks nearing the village from the south.

In one leap, Gabe settled behind Izaak. Hero's ears flattened, his legs danced.

Izaak stroked the stallion's neck. "We'll save you," he whispered.

Gabe took the reins and steered the horse past the farm and into the fields. Izaak bounced, trying to find his balance. If it hadn't been for Gabe's body firm against his back and Gabe's arms around him holding the reins, Izaak was sure he would have fallen off the horse right away.

"There's Albert mending the fence," Izaak said, panting as he tried to balance with the rhythm of the horse's movements.

"The Germans are coming," Izaak shouted at Albert, who watched them with questioning eyes.

Albert waved at them. "Go!" he shouted.

# Friendship

"Hold on tight," Gabe grunted behind him. "We're going to speed up."

Izaak gripped the mane tightly and tried to move his body with Hero's. In the distance loomed the sea dike. Not the real sea dike, he knew, but the middle one of three dikes to protect the land from the sea. This dike was called the dreamer.

For the next fifteen minutes, Izaak tried to do several things at the same time. He needed to remember to dig in his knees and to hold on to Hero's mane. Hero's trot made Izaak bounce up and down like a ball. Gabe's arms folded around him, keeping him on the horse.

Once they entered the path to the dike, Gabe spurred Hero into a gallop. Now Izaak felt as if he would fly over the horse's neck. He gripped the mane until his hands felt numb. The wind pulled his hair. Flecks of white foam blew from Hero's mouth into Izaak's face.

The horse's muscles beneath him surged with power. His heart raced. They had to succeed, he thought. They had to.

They reached the foot of the dike. "Whoa," Gabe shouted. Hero slowed down.

Izaak turned his head and looked back at the farm.

Gabe dismounted and helped Izaak off the horse. Izaak's legs trembled so badly that they almost buckled. Gabe led Hero by the bridle up the slope of the dike. Until they reached the other side, they would be visible from quite a distance.

Once below the dike, Hero started nibbling on the first new sprigs of grass.

Izaak looked at Gabe. "Why is this dike called the dreamer?"

"There are three dikes." Gabe said. "The sleeper. The dreamer." He patted the ground they were sitting on. "The next one," he said, pointing at the dike ahead of them, "is the watcher. The watcher is the highest and has to protect the land from the sea," Gabe said. "Now, crawl to the top, but stay low."

Izaak squinted in the direction of the farm. Three military trucks were driving down the road from the village. Izaak crawled down, his face white with fear. "Three trucks," he said.

"Stay down," Gabe said. "For now, we're safe."

Izaak and Gabe sat down in the grass.

"If the Germans find us ... ," Gabe took a deep breath. "They'll take Annie and you and me away and send Uncle Piet and Aunt Anna to a concentration camp."

Izaak nodded. The older boys at school had talked about it one day. A family that lived close to the church had been taken away. Izaak paused. A father, mother and four children had been sent to a concentration camp because they were hiding a Jew.

"Where is your family?" Izaak had wondered about Gabe and his family, but had been afraid to ask. Today he felt that he could.

"My family was in hiding on a farm in the next town, over there." Gabe pointed to the east and stared into the distance. "The farmer raised and trained prize-winning Frisian horses." He pointed at Hero.

Izaak watched Gabe's face. The older boy seemed so far away.

"One day I took Marijke to a neighboring farm to help with the haying." He paused as if he had to think what happened next.

"When we returned at night, they were gone." Gabe stood up. He thrust his hands in his pockets.

"The farmer, his wife, my mother, father and three sisters. Gone!" His voice rose. He paced the grass. Back and forth. Back and forth. "They're all in some camp either in Poland or Germany!" He screamed now. "They're probably murdered by the Nazis! And only because we're Jews!" Tears streamed down his face.

Izaak's heart hurt. The ball in his stomach tightened. He wanted to touch Gabe, but his body wouldn't move.

"I hate being a Jew." Gabe fell on his knees. He pounded the earth with his fists. "I hate it! I hate everything!" His sobs were long, shaking his entire body.

Izaak held his breath. Hero grazed beside him. He couldn't believe what Gabe had said. Did he hate being a Jew? No, but being a Jew had brought him here and made him miss his family.

Papa had always told him he should be proud to be Jewish. But Gabe made him doubt Papa's words.

Izaak didn't know how long they stayed behind the dike. Time was filled with thoughts and fear. Any moment he expected a fierce-looking soldier with a rifle to peer over the dike.

"I don't know where my family is." Izaak didn't know if Gabe heard.

Gabe looked at him. His face was swollen and the one side looked even more purple than usual, but it didn't scare Izaak anymore.

"I know," Gabe said. He wiped his face on the sleeve of his farmer's jacket. "But the Germans will not take Hero." Gabe's voice sounded angry.

"Why do they want Hero? He's not Jewish." Izaak didn't understand.

Gabe smiled. "No. The Germans want to use him in the war because he's strong and healthy."

"They'll never get him." Izaak balled his fists.

"The Germans sent Uncle Piet a letter, ordering him to hand over the horse. Once, the Germans came to the farm, but that day Hero was at the blacksmith in the village. We sent Annie to tell the smith to keep the horse till dark."

Izaak let out a sigh. He refused to think what would have happened if Hero hadn't been at the blacksmith.

"Uncle Piet brought the horse back when it was dark. From that time on we've tried to hide Hero as much as possible. We took him to the blacksmith once as a precaution, but the Germans never came."

He motioned Izaak to the top of the dike.

Izaak crawled up the grassy slope, lay on his stomach and peered in the direction of the farm. His eyes narrowed into slits as he observed the farm buildings. All of a sudden he spotted a figure walking in the fields. Was it a soldier? No, there would have been more than one. He watched for a few moments more. When he turned around, Gabe was lying on his stomach beside Hero.

Izaak turned back to his task. The wind chilled his body. He shivered, but kept his eyes on the lonely figure in the fields as it drew closer. At last Izaak recognized Albert.

"Gabe!" Izaak called down. "It's Albert!"

Slowly, Gabe got to his feet and joined him. Side by side they watched Albert come to the dike, until they felt it safe enough to wave at him.

"It's all right. You can come home."

Gabe tugged at his sleeve. "Go get Hero."

For a moment Izaak stared at Gabe. Then he rushed down the slope.

Hero looked up and neighed.

Izaak ruffled Hero's mane and pressed his own nose against Hero's. "I told you we would save you," he whispered. Then he took the bridle and coached Hero up the slope. "Come, Hero. You can do it." Gabe and Albert stood on top of the dike.

"Here. I'll give you a hand up." Gabe smiled at him. "Hold onto the reins."

Izaak grabbed hold of the reins and dug his heels into Hero's warm sides. He swayed gently as Hero walked beside the men.

Albert looked up at Izaak. "That was quite the rescue. Who thought of that brilliant idea?"

Gabe smiled. "Jan here."

"Did the soldiers come?" Izaak asked.

"Yes," Albert answered. "The three of you went over the dike just as I heard the trucks. I went to the kitchen to find Piet. He was worried like crazy. He had no idea how Gabe and the horse could have disappeared."

Izaak's heart pounded. "He didn't know about me?"

"No. When I told him, he grinned."

Izaak felt so tall, looking at the world from Hero's back. "What did he do when the soldiers came? Did they take the other two?"

"Since when do you talk so much?" Albert pulled at his cap and smiled at Izaak.

Izaak's face burned.

"The soldiers searched the barn and the stables, but didn't go into the living quarters, which surprised us. They asked about *der Hengst*, the stallion, and Piet knew they meant Hero. He told them the horse had been stolen a couple of weeks ago. At first they didn't believe him, but after they'd searched everywhere, they left. They were not interested in the mares, just the stallion."

A great weight slid off Izaak's shoulders. Gabe looked at him and patted his knee. A warm feeling entered his chest.

# No Escape

"Tomorrow the horses will stay outside all night as well. The weather is warm enough." Gabe lifted one of Marijke's hind legs and brushed the long hairs down.

"You mean we won't bring them inside anymore?" Izaak copied Gabe's actions on one of Hero's hind legs. "How will we protect them?" He let go of the leg and leaned against the warm body.

"The war's over. It's a matter of days. The Germans are not interested in horses anymore. They have to save their own hides." Gabe stood up and peered over the horse's back. "The Germans are fleeing. The troops are disorganized. They have no food and haven't been paid in weeks. Don't you remember what they said on the radio last night?"

Izaak nodded. He could hardly believe that the war was really going to be over. No more hiding from the German soldiers. But most important — the thought sent shivers up his spine — he would be able to find his family. At least he hoped so.

Gabe stopped brushing. "Listen."

Izaak put down Hero's leg. "I don't hear anything," he said. He listened again.

Gabe stepped away from Hero and walked over to the door to the barn, opened it and walked in.

As Izaak followed, his ears caught the sound of engines. Motorcycles. German motorcycles. His heart froze. Panic gripped him. "We have to hide!" Izaak screamed. "We have to hide Hero!"

Gabe clenched his fists. "What are they doing here? It's too late to hide Hero. Quick, climb into the trough and I'll cover you with hay."

"What if the soldiers use pitchforks to check the trough?"

"They won't!" Gabe screamed. "Get in!"

"What about you? Where will you hide?" Izaak's voice was shrill with fear.

"I don't know." Gabe seemed lost for words. "It's too late. We're all going to die anyway. You have to hide, Jan!"

"I won't." Izaak had made up his mind. "If the Germans are going to take Hero, they'll have to take me too. I know how to take care of him." He felt calm now.

"No, you don't. Come here. I'll give you an up!"

Izaak glared at Gabe. "NO!"

Gabe raced around Marijke and stood in front of Izaak. They didn't speak.

The sound of the engines droned closer.

Izaak kept both feet on the ground.

Gabe took a step towards him. He lifted his arm, brush in hand.

Izaak stared at Gabe. He breathed hard, his eyes big.

Something heavy hit the side of Izaak's head. His head spun. The sound of the engines drowned out the scents and sounds of the stable. He tried to focus. Blackness cloaked him as he felt himself being lifted.


Soft and sharp sticks tickled Izaak's nose. He moved his arm. Hay. He was lying in a heap of hay. A sharp pain shot through his head. For a moment, he lay still. One by one, the events came back to him. His heart pounded.

The Germans. Hero. Gabe with the brush in his hand.

Izaak listened. Muffled voices came through the stable door. Holding his head,

Izaak sat up. Hay covered his head and body. He didn't bother wiping it off.

He stared at the three empty stalls. Hero, Marijke and Clasina were gone. So was Gabe.

His limbs trembling, Izaak climbed over the iron bars of the trough. With a soft thud, he landed in the straw below. Trying not to make a sound, he padded to the door. It stood ajar.

The barn doors were open too. Outside, he spotted four soldiers with rifles, one of Uncle Piet's wagons and the behinds of three familiar horses.

He heard Uncle Piet's voice. "You're not taking all my horses. I need them for the haying and I need the wagon. Marijke here," he pointed at the horse in the middle, "is having a foal."

Izaak didn't understand what the Germans were saying. He crept out of the stables and into the barn, staying close to the wall so the soldiers couldn't see him.

Through the gap beside the hinges of the barn door he spotted Gabe. Gabe was holding Marijke and Hero by their bits. Albert held onto Clasina's.

From the doorway of the small house, Nel and the children watched the events at the barn.

Again Izaak heard Uncle Piet say, "I need those horses!"

The German's reply sounded angry.

Izaak noticed the soldier's black leather boots. The war was supposed to be over.

The boots marched over to Gabe.

Izaak's heart froze. Now they're going to find out Gabe is a Jew, he thought.

"If you take the horses," Gabe's voice trembled, "you have to take me too."

"Gabe, no!" Uncle Piet stepped forward.

A soldier grabbed Uncle Piet from behind and pulled him back.

More soldiers talked.

Izaak didn't understand a word they said. The ball in his stomach rolled.

To Izaak's surprise another soldier

grabbed Marijke by the bridle. He turned the horse around and handed her to Uncle Piet.

Izaak pressed his fists into his stomach. Had they changed their minds? Were they not taking the horses?

In the next moment, a command was given. The soldier let go of Uncle Piet, allowing him to take Marijke's bridle. Uncle Piet's hands trembled as he stroked the horse's nose.

The soldier motioned to harness Clasina and Hero. Albert went into the barn and grabbed the harnesses from a hook on the wall.

Izaak held his breath, but Albert never noticed him. As he watched Albert harnessing the horses, his eyes caught a movement down the farm lane. In horror he watched a group of soldiers running towards the farm. As they came closer Izaak noticed how dirty and tired they looked. He counted eight.

Gabe's face was tense with strain and fear. He turned and took the reins.

Hero turned his head towards the barn door. His nostrils flared.

Izaak's breath caught. He could have sworn that Hero looked straight at him.

A command was given and the soldiers climbed onto the flatbed of the wagon. Gabe took his seat, speaking comforting words to the horses. Hearing the command, the horses strained forward and pulled the wagon. Two German soldiers mounted their motorcycles; two others took the passenger seat. The engines revved. Followed by the motorcycles the wagon rode down the lane in the direction of the village.

Izaak's heart swelled and tears ran down his face. He would never forget the image of Hero, Clasina and Gabe driving a wagon full of soldiers.

Hero trotted with pride, his head held high, his mane blowing to one side. Izaak watched until they reached the end of the lane, turned into the village and disappeared from sight.

# Liberation

Footsteps coming from the house made Izaak look up. Aunt Anna, followed by Annie, came running. Out of breath, Aunt Anna kneeled beside him.

"Jan," she cried softly. "What's going on? I thought this war was over."

"Gabe," Izaak tried to swallow his tears. "Gabe went with the soldiers. They're going to kill him."

Aunt Anna pulled him to his feet. "What happened?"

Izaak looked up at Aunt Anna. "It was all my fault."

"I don't believe that," she said. "Let's find the others."

Together they walked outside to meet Uncle Piet and Albert.

"Jan!" Jaap's cry of joy startled Izaak. "Where were you hiding?"

His face flustered, Izaak looked at the people he'd known only for six months, but who had become like family. They gathered around Uncle Piet and Marijke. His eyes met Uncle Piet's. "What's going to happen to them? Will they come back?"

Silence followed. Everyone looked at the ground.

"We don't know, Jan. We don't know." Uncle Piet's voice was flat and defeated.

"They're on the run, you know." Albert pointed at the village. "The Germans are fleeing."

"But why are they taking the horses now?" Izaak's lip trembled.

"They're taking everything in their path. Bicycles. Wagons. Anything."

"What good will that do?" Uncle Piet's voice was low.

"They're scared and they're panicking." Albert walked over to Marijke. "Shall I put her in her stable? She's shaking."

Izaak watched the trembling mare, swollen with her foal.

Uncle Piet nodded and handed the mare's lead to Albert.

"What will they do to Gabe?" Aunt Anna clenched her fists.

Nobody said a word.


That night, Izaak tossed and turned. Over and over he saw the image of Gabe, driving the wagon full of German soldiers into the village pulled by two proud Frisian horses, followed by two Germans on motorcycles. Oh, Hero, he thought.

The next morning, as the small troupe walked to school, the twins didn't fight like they usually did. Annie walked beside Izaak. She didn't say a word.

Once they reached the school yard they felt the excitement.

Johannes, a boy from grade six, came running down to meet them. "The Canadians are coming! We will be free!"

Too late, Izaak thought. They came one day too late.

Miss Afke had a hard time settling the students.

"Today, April 14, 1945, is an important day for our village," she wrote with chalk on the blackboard.

"The Canadian troops and the Dutch Interior Army have managed to come from the south and the east into our province to liberate our village," she said, when she finally had her students' attention. She pointed out the route they had taken on the large map that hung at the front of the class. "They're expected to liberate all of Friesland in the next few days."

The class cheered.

"Why are the Germans fleeing west?" Nel, a big girl two seats ahead of Izaak, had put up her hand. "They should go east to Germany instead."

"They can't," Miss Afke explained. "The Canadian army has cut them off. The western provinces have not been liberated yet and that's why they're fleeing west."

"I hope they chase them all into the North Sea, so they can drown." The quiet boy who'd come to the school after Izaak spoke up. The whole class turned towards him. It was the first time he'd said anything.

Miss Afke cleared her throat. "As soon as the rest of the country is liberated, we might lose some of our friends," she said. "They might go back home."

With a shock, Izaak realized he hadn't even thought of that. He had been so preoccupied with Hero and Gabe that he hadn't even thought of his parents and Sarah now that the war was over.

Would they be able to live together in their house with the bright rooms? He was afraid to think of it. He had heard so many stories of Jewish people killed by the Germans.

*Ra-ta-ta-taaa-ta-taa.* The music of a band drew them all from their seats.

Miss Afke was already opening the door. The children tumbled out and stared as a marching band appeared down Main Street.

"School is over for the day." The headmaster was jumping up and down in excitement. "Go home! Celebrate!"

Jaap and Annie stood beside Izaak. Behind the band followed a Canadian soldier on a BSA motorcycle. Izaak had never seen such a bike. Canadian and Dutch flags decorated the big Sherman tanks that followed. People were so excited that they had climbed on top of the tanks. The soldiers waved and sang. The whole population of the little village was dancing in the street. Already, the red, white and blue flags were flying from houses and atop the steeple of the church.

Jaap could hardly contain himself. "I'm going on one of those tanks," he shouted. "Come on, Jan!" In the next few moments, Izaak was pulled high onto a Canadian tank by two young soldiers. They put a Canadian flag in his hand and the liberation bug bit him. He waved eagerly at the people along the street.

Just outside the village, Jaap and Izaak got off the tank, hands full of chocolate bars and packages of chewing gum. Annie had followed the tank. Together they ran home, where Aunt Anna had baked a cake in celebration.

"Will Jan and I go home now?" Annie asked with her mouth full of cake.

"The part of Holland where your parents are in hiding has not been liberated yet." Aunt Anna looked from Annie to Izaak. "We hope the rest of the country will be free soon."

The mood around the table grew somber. They all thought of the families who were still in hiding, and of Clasina, Hero and Gabe.

After a week of celebration, school began again. Izaak was glad. There was much work to do on the farm, but everything there reminded him of Gabe and Hero. At school, his mind went somewhere else.

Izaak had taken over the task of looking after Marijke since Gabe was gone. Uncle Piet worried about the mare. She hadn't been herself since the Germans had stolen Clasina and Hero.

One night Izaak stayed with Marijke until Uncle Piet came looking for him.

"Marijke is restless." Izaak stroked the mane and neck of the mare. She whinnied when she heard Uncle Piet's voice. They had made a small corral in a corner of the barn, so Marijke would have lots of space when she went into labor.

"Give her some extra straw," Uncle Piet said. "I have the feeling she might foal during the night."

"Can I stay with her?" Izaak pleaded.

"We'll both stay with her." Uncle Piet placed two bales of straw beside the gate of the small enclosure and they made themselves comfortable.

"It could be a long wait, Jan." Uncle Piet yawned.

Izaak must have dozed off. He woke with a start when Uncle Piet called his name and he heard Marijke's soft neighing.

"The foal. Jan, look!"

Izaak rubbed his eyes. A tiny horse was trying to stand up on spindly legs. Marijke was licking its shiny, wet coat.

"It's so small," Izaak gasped. "I've never seen a newborn foal before."

"It's a she. A filly." Uncle Piet stroked Marijke's mane. The mare neighed, her ears flattened.

"She's protective of her young," Uncle Piet said.

Izaak stared.

"She's Hero's daughter," Uncle Piet went on. "We have to think of a suitable name for her."

Izaak's brain searched for a name that would remind them of Hero. Heress, like princess, or Hera. "Hera," he said out loud.

Uncle Piet smiled at him. "The perfect name! Hera was a Greek goddess, the queen of the gods, and the name means protector."

Wow! Uncle Piet knew all about Greek mythology, just like Papa. Izaak's throat closed. Papa, he thought. If only Papa could be here in the stable with him. He turned away.

In the following days, Izaak's mind and body were filled with the responsibility for Marijke and Hera. He watched the filly drink from her mother. He watched her try to frolic and dance on wobbly legs. He loved her soft neighing and the feel of her tender lips when she licked his hand.

On May 5, 1945, the rest of the country celebrated its liberation from five hard years of German occupation.

# The Great Reunion

After more celebrations, life on the farm slowly became more normal.

"Will my parents be free?" Annie asked Aunt Anna while she helped clear the table.

"If they are alive, we should hear from them soon." Aunt Anna looked from Annie to Izaak.

A strange feeling overcame Izaak. Lately, he often thought about his parents and Sarah. He hoped they had survived the cold winter in Amsterdam. He knew that many people had died from starvation.

What would happen if they didn't come back? The tightness in his stomach had returned. The ball in his stomach rolled and some days he couldn't eat. At night his thoughts grew into monsters and kept him awake.

Annie's parents appeared one afternoon near the end of May. They had survived the war by hiding in the chicken coop of a farm in one of the eastern provinces. The reunion with their little girl moved everyone to smiles and tears. Izaak had to leave the room.

Aunt Anna followed him to the pasture where Marijke and Hera were grazing.

"Wait, Jan!" she called.

Izaak didn't wait. He climbed on top of the wooden gate and stared at the horse and filly without seeing them.

Aunt Anna climbed beside him and put her arm around his shoulder. "I know what you're feeling and you're right, we haven't heard from them. It depends on where your parents were, but as soon as they are out of hiding, they will start to look for you. I know." She squeezed his shoulder. "They might have our address, but no means of transportation. We are a free country, but not everything is back to normal, Jan."

All Izaak could do was stare. His throat was in knots and the words couldn't get out. His mind filled with doubts and fear.

"No matter what happens, Jan. You will always have a home." Aunt Anna touched his face. She climbed down the fence and retraced her steps to the farm.

The house was quiet without Annie and Gabe. Izaak was glad that Jaap came often, and they both did chores for Uncle Piet.

June followed May. One evening, the sun set in an orange fireball and the sky held a red glow.

"An evening sky dressed in red will bring sunshine when you get out of bed," was Aunt Anna's saying. Jaap had gone home and Izaak was back in his spot on the wooden gate. He watched the cows in the far pastures, chewing their cud, their black and white bodies dotting the land. Thin ribbons of mist rose from the ditches, fencing in the pastures. The quiet of the evening reached the far horizon.

Just ahead of him, Marijke nuzzled her young. Without warning, her head shot up and she let out a longing neigh that reached the horizon. Izaak listened. Did he imagine it ... or did he hear an answer to that yearning call.

His heart skipped and he held his breath. From the south, the evening breeze blew the answer to Marijke's neigh. The mare's ears moved and she returned the call.

Izaak jumped down from the gate. He stood still. Marijke came to stand beside him on the other side of the gate. Izaak scanned the road to the village, but there was no sign of a horse.

They waited. Marijke and Izaak. He

heard the mare's breathing. Her nostrils flared. She stepped nervously from one foot to the other.

Izaak's heart swelled when he heard the faint *clip-clop* of a horse on the road. Now his eyes spotted a rider and horse coming down the road to the village. The horse was black. As it neared, Izaak noticed the powerful gallop that could only be one animal.

Joy exploded in Izaak's chest as he recognized the rider. "Hero!" he shouted. "Gabe!" Izaak's cries awoke the small house at the end of the farm. The door opened. First Albert, then Nel and all the children came running outside.

Izaak couldn't move. He had to hold onto the wooden railing of the gate. "Jaap," he cried, "call Uncle Piet and Aunt Anna!"

Finally, Gabe and Hero stopped in front of him. Izaak laughed and cried at the same time. He touched Gabe and Hero, stroking the mane of the powerful stallion.

As soon as Gabe dismounted, Uncle Piet and Aunt Anna came running, their faces wet with tears. Aunt Anna threw her arms around Gabe, and Uncle Piet took Hero's bridle.

"You both have lost weight," Aunt Anna cried, "but you're alive!"

Uncle Piet thrust his face into the horse's mane. Nobody spoke.

After feeding, Hero was reunited with Marijke and the filly. The two horses nuzzled each other's manes. Hero walked around Marijke, while the mare stood still, Hera close at her side. The stallion touched the foal's back with his nostrils. Then Hero turned and galloped across the pasture and back. He halted in front of his family and lowered his head to the grass. Marijke grazed as well while Hera darted around her.

When they were all seated around the kitchen table, Gabe finally had a chance to tell them about his adventures. "The Germans were so scared, they never cared if I was a Jew or not,"

Gabe said. "As long as I looked after the horses, they left me alone. I had to look after ten horses."

Izaak watched his friend admiringly. "Weren't you afraid?"

"Not when I noticed how scared they were." Gabe laughed. "In North Holland they got into heavy fighting with the Allied troops, and I managed to get away with three horses." Gabe took a deep breath. He wasn't used to talking so much, Izaak thought.

"I couldn't travel with three horses, so I left Clasina and the other horse with a farmer, who will take good care of them. We can get Clasina later. Hero and I traveled all the way around the Ijssel Meer to get back to Friesland. At night we stayed at farms. Sometimes we stayed for a few days and helped the farmer with the haying." He looked at the faces around the kitchen table. "It took us four weeks to get back here."

Uncle Piet's eyes filled. "You are a hero," he said.

"No," Gabe said. "It was Jan. Jan is the hero. He wanted to go with Hero when the Germans came."

Izaak's face colored.

"But I couldn't let him do that. And I didn't want the Germans to find him and that's why ... " Gabe looked at Izaak. "How is your head?"

Izaak smiled. "It was only black and yellow for three weeks."

"I'm not sorry." Gabe laughed. They all laughed with joy and with relief.

"After I knocked Jan out and covered him with hay in the trough, I took all three horses outside, so the Germans didn't need to go into the stable and search."

A warm feeling glowed in Izaak's chest. Gabe had protected him till the end.

That night Izaak tossed and turned again. It was a miracle that Gabe and Hero had survived the ordeal, but Izaak still waited for one more miracle.

When Jaap and Izaak were cleaning

up the yard behind the barn a few days later, a cyclist came down the lane to the farm.

They both halted their work and watched. As the person neared, they saw that it was an old woman, riding a rusty bike. Her hair was gray and tied in a bun. Her cheekbones stuck out and her face was lined like parchment paper.

But something in her eyes caught Izaak's breath. She dismounted and took a second to find her balance. Her eyes found Izaak's.

Izaak's lips barely moved. "Mama."

"Izaak!" She stumbled closer.

Izaak ran and caught her before her knees buckled. She didn't weigh much.

"Mama," was all he could bring out. He didn't notice that Jaap had disappeared until Aunt Anna came running out of the barn.

Aunt Anna helped Izaak walk his mother inside the kitchen.

Mama finally found her voice. "I can't believe how much you've grown," she said. Her lip quivered.

And Izaak couldn't believe how old and small his mother looked.

"I will leave you two alone," Aunt Anna said after she had buttered a piece of bread and put a cup of hot tea in front of Mama.

Izaak didn't know what to say. Mama just looked at him.

"I can't tell you how often I have thought of this moment." She wiped her eyes with the back of her hand. "Even when ... " She paused. "After you left, I found a hiding place in an old warehouse that had been boarded up. A young woman brought me food. There was no heat in the winter."

Izaak shivered. He couldn't imagine how Mama had survived the cold. And she was so thin. He didn't think the woman had brought her much food. He had so many questions, but they all stuck in his throat.

The ball in Izaak's stomach started rolling. He had imagined their reunion many times, but it had never been like this.

"Papa and Sarah were found in their hiding place and sent to a camp." Mama swallowed hard. "They have not come back yet, but I have hope that soon they will return."

Izaak sat still.

"Every day people return from the camps," Mama whispered.

Izaak held onto his stomach. In a swift movement he stood up, opened the kitchen door and ran outside.

Beside the wooden gate, the ball left his stomach and he threw up. Tears flooded for Papa and Sarah wherever they might be.

A soft nudge made Izaak look up. Hero caressed his hair with his lips.

"Oh, Hero," Izaak sighed and pulled the animal's head down. His tears ran down Hero's face. "Where are they?" he whispered.

Izaak didn't return to the farm for the evening meal.

Gabe joined him after. "Not hungry?" he asked.

"No." Izaak looked at his friend. "Have you heard from your family?"

"No." Gabe stood beside him. Together they stared ahead, silent.

The sun set in a colorless haze. Gabe walked back to the farm. Izaak followed him inside and went straight to bed.

Izaak's mother stayed on the farm for a week. She had to build up the strength to bicycle back to Amsterdam.

Finally, Izaak and Mama stood outside, packed and ready. Their saddlebags were filled with food to take back to a tiny flat that Mama had found for the two of them before she had come to the farm.

Izaak was not so sure about going back to Amsterdam.

He said good-bye to the Ademas. "I'll miss you, Jaap." Izaak's throat felt thick.

Jaap nodded and pumped Izaak's hand.

"We'd like you and your mother to spend your summers on the farm." Aunt Anna held onto Izaak's arm. "But first you have to get settled in your home."

Mama hugged Aunt Anna.

Uncle Piet patted Izaak's shoulder. "I can use some help this summer." His voice was hoarse.

Gabe stood at Izaak's favorite wooden gate.

Izaak ran over and threw his arms around the boy he admired so much.

"I'll be back," he said through his tears.

Gabe nodded.

Then they were on their way. As they rode to the village, Izaak looked back. Gabe had mounted Hero. The stallion galloped to the end of the pasture. Gabe's hand went up. Hero neighed. Izaak waved. The rider and stallion blurred together.

His heroes.

# Author's Note

*Hero* is a work of fiction based on true events during World War II.

The stallion Held (Hero) is a real horse that belonged to my great uncle Jan Hoogterp. On the eve of the liberation of the province of Friesland, the stallion was taken by fleeing German soldiers. Seventeen-year-old Andries Hofstee, farmhand and Held's caretaker, vowed never to leave his beloved stallion alone. Andries and Held drove a wagon full of German soldiers west over the Afsluitdijk into North Holland. Andries and Held were able to escape during heavy fighting. They wandered for a month from farm to farm until the whole country was liberated, after which they returned to my great uncle's farm.

During my research on the couriers, girls and women who worked for the resistance during World War II, I learned that many Jewish children were taken from Amsterdam to farms in Friesland by young girls sometimes on the carriers of their bikes. These children went to school, disguised as nieces and nephews of the farmer and his family. After the war some children were reunited with their families, but in a few known instances, when the Jewish parents had perished, the farm family adopted the child.

Germany invaded the Netherlands on May 10, 1940. Life became difficult for the Dutch citizens, especially the Jewish people. As the war progressed Jews lost their jobs, were forbidden to walk in parks and ride buses. Schools were closed for Jewish children. On their outer garments they had to sew a yellow star with the word *Jood* (Jew) printed on it. Later, their property and possessions were taken and they were ordered to live in a ghetto in Amsterdam. From the ghetto a train left once a week to transport Jews to the Dutch concentration camp, Westerbork. In this camp the Jewish prisoners waited for further transportation to camps in Germany and Poland. The first transport from Westerbork to Poland happened on July 15, 1942.

Many Jews disobeyed the orders and went into hiding. Dutch people risked their lives to transport and hide Jewish people. In July 1942, Piet Meerburg, a student from Amsterdam, traveled to Friesland to find safe homes for Jewish children. As a result, the involvement of the resistance movement in saving Jewish people, especially children, increased.

The war lasted five years. The winter of 1944–1945 was called the "Hunger Winter" as so many people died of starvation in the big cities. It was also one of the coldest winters, and without fuel to heat their homes, the Dutch people suffered terribly.

For more information on World War II and Friesland and for the study guide, please visit my web site at: www.marthaattema.com

Photo credit: M.J. Hughes

*Hero* is  martha sttema's second Young Reader about World War II. Her first was *Daughter of Light* (Orca, 2001). Hero was a real stallion owned by Martha's great uncle and stolen by the Germans just as the war was ending. A boy from the farm went with the horse and managed to escape and bring Hero home. In *Hero*, truth becomes powerful fiction. Martha's next project involves building instead of writing. She and her husband are building a straw bale house, which will be both their home and an educational site.

Other books by martha attema:

*A Time to Choose*
*A Light in the Dunes*
*Daughter of Light*
*When the War is Over*